D1238047

THE BIGGEST BUBBLE IN THE WORLD

by Janet Lorimer
illustrated by Diane Paterson

An Easy-Read Story Book

Franklin Watts
New York/London/Toronto/Sydney
1982

R.L. 2.7 Spache Revised Formula

Library of Congress Cataloging in Publication Data

Lorimer, Janet.
The biggest bubble in the world.

(An Easy-read story book)
Summary: Harvey and Jeremy blow a huge sticky
bubble that bounces through town picking up everything in its path.
[1. Bubbles—Fiction.   2. Bubble gum—Fiction]
I. Paterson, Diane, 1946–   ill.   II. Title.
III. Series.
PZ7.L8867Bi   81-21941
ISBN 0-531-04378-9 AACR2

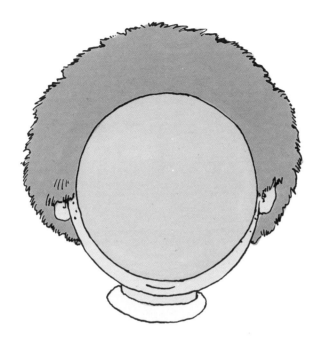

For my daughters,
Kerry and Marnie,
whose knowledge of
and experience with
bubble gum
proved an invaluable aid

Harvey raced into Jeremy's yard, shouting, "Guess what's happening this Saturday?"

"That's the first day of the County Fair," Jeremy said.

"Right!" said Harvey. "I've got this great idea! There's going to be a bubble-gum-blowing contest. Whoever blows the biggest bubble wins ten dollars. We're going to win!"

"What makes you think we're going to win?" asked Jeremy.

"That's easy," Harvey laughed. "First we're going to chew a lot of bubble gum. I just bought us four dollars worth and—"

"That's four hundred pieces of gum!" yelped Jeremy. "Where did you get that much money?"

"My grandmother gave it to me for my birthday," Harvey said.

"Your mom's going to be mad when she finds out you spent it all on bubble gum," Jeremy said.

"No, she won't. Not when we win ten dollars. Now be quiet and listen to my great plan. After we chew all the gum, we make a big gum ball and blow it up."

"With what?" Jeremy asked.

"With your tire pump, what else? Here, start chewing."

The boys had three days to chew all the gum. They chewed and chewed and chewed some more. They chewed in school and got caught. They chewed at home until everything began to taste like bubble gum.

"You'd better stop chewing that gum," Jeremy's mother said. "It'll pull all your teeth out. You'll be the only kid in the third grade with false teeth."

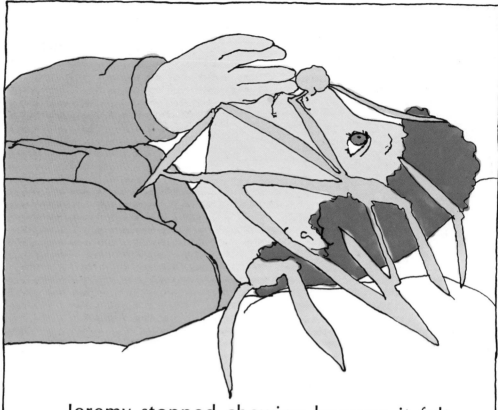

Jeremy stopped chewing because it felt so good to stop. But that night he thought about all the gum he still had.

After the lights were out he popped a piece of gum into his mouth and started chewing. When he woke up next morning there was gum in his hair, gum in his ear, and gum all over the pillow.

By Saturday morning, the boys had chewed all the gum. Harvey raced to Jeremy's house right after breakfast. They wadded the gum into a big ball and stuck it on the end of the tire pump.

Harvey started to pump. He pumped and pumped, but nothing happened.

"It isn't going to work," Jeremy said.

"That's because we aren't strong enough. Wow, this is going to be the world's biggest bubble!" grinned Harvey.

"It isn't going to be anything but a big blob," Jeremy grumbled. "This is a dumb idea."

"Hey, we aren't going to give up that easily," Harvey said. "Let's take it to the gas station and use the air hose!"

·Harvey put the wad of gum on the end of the air hose and pushed the lever. It worked! The wad of gum turned into a bubble. It got bigger and bigger.

"Shut the air off before it pops!" Jeremy gasped.

Harvey just stood there with his mouth open, staring at the bubble. It was as big as a house and still growing.

"Hey, what're you kids doing?" yelled the attendant.

Harvey shut off the hose and pinched the end of the bubble to hold in the air. "Come on! We've got to get to that contest," he said.

Just as Harvey pulled the bubble away from the air hose, a big gust of wind blew it out of his hand. The bubble went bouncing down the street.

"Stop that bubble!" yelled Harvey.

"It's going to pop!" Jeremy shouted. The boys ran after the bubble.

But the bubble didn't pop! It just bounced down the street. It was so sticky everything stuck to it. It picked up old newspapers, bottle caps, and rocks. It flew past an old lady and grabbed her umbrella. The lady ran after the bubble.

It bounced past the minister and grabbed his hat. The minister ran after the bubble, too.

Then it rolled over a cat. "Oh, no!" groaned Jeremy. "That cat will pop the bubble!" But the cat just stuck to the bubble.

"Look at that!" Harvey shouted to Jeremy. "We've got half the town following us. We're lucky that bubble is going in the right direction."

The bubble bounced and rolled along like a big pink balloon. Suddenly it stopped! It hung in the air as if it couldn't decide which way to go.

"Oh, oh!" whispered Jeremy. "What's that crazy bubble going to do?"

"Look out!" shouted Harvey. "Here it comes!"

The bubble flew right at them. Jeremy and Harvey jumped backward, right against the minister who fell over the old lady.

Everyone fell down like a row of dominoes. There were arms and legs sticking out in all directions.

The bubble sailed right over them. Just as Harvey got someone's elbow out of his ear, the bubble flew back again.

"Duck!" yelled Jeremy. Everyone fell flat again. The bubble sailed over their heads and up into the air. It flew right over the houses and trees.

"Come on," said Harvey. "We can cut through the alley and catch that bubble on Main Street."

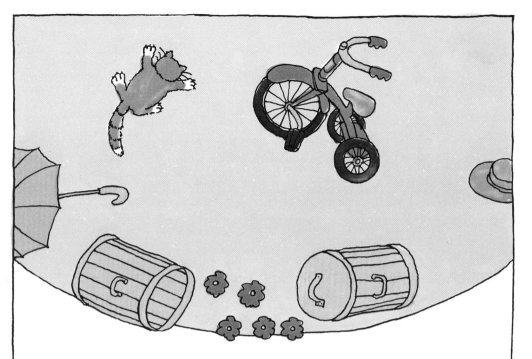

There were more things sticking to it now. A tricycle, all the flowers from a flower bed, and two trash cans that banged and clanked everytime it bounced.

"It sure looks funny," Harvey giggled.

Nobody else thought it was funny. The crowd of people chasing that bubble was growing.

But the bubble wouldn't stop. On it flew!

Then Jeremy heard something he didn't want to hear. It was a parade coming up Main Street! The traffic policeman saw the bubble. He put up his hand and blew his whistle, but the bubble ran right over him. It took his whistle, his hat, and all the brass buttons on his uniform. The policeman began chasing the bubble, too.

The marchers in the parade all ran into each other trying to get away from the big bubble. But it rolled right down the middle of the parade, snatching a tuba, a drum, and three trumpets. It even grabbed the baton right out of the baton twirler's hand.

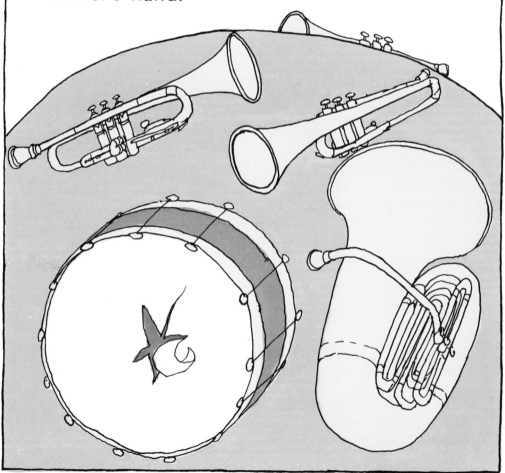

Harvey and Jeremy looked at each other. "I think maybe we're in trouble," Harvey yelled.

Before Jeremy could answer, the bubble bounced by a man coming out of the bank and stole a bag of money from him.

"I *know* we're in trouble," Jeremy panted.

"Well, it can't get any worse," Harvey yelled.

"Yes it can," Jeremy shouted. "Listen!"

Someone had heard all the noise and called the fire department. The boys heard the siren. Then they saw the big red fire truck turn onto Main Street. The fire truck was racing toward the bubble and the bubble was racing toward the fire truck. Closer and closer, together they came!

Harvey was so scared his freckles almost jumped off his nose! The people chasing the bubble all stopped and covered their ears! Jeremy shut his eyes tight! He could not bear to watch. But he heard the terrible POP, BANG, CLANK, CRASH when the fire truck collided with the bubble, trashcans, trumpets, brass buttons, tricycle, bottle caps, whistle, and cat!

Very slowly Jeremy opened one eye. Oh, boy, he and Harvey were definitely in big, *big* trouble!

The boys didn't win the bubble gum contest, but the man coming out of the bank was a robber. Jeremy and Harvey got a reward for catching him.

The reward money paid for all the damages and Harvey and Jeremy spent two weeks scraping gum off things.

On Jeremy's first day of freedom, he was playing in his yard with his little sister. When she got angry, she would bite, but Jeremy figured she was a lot safer to be with than Harvey!

Jeremy heard a shout and looked up. Harvey raced into the yard.

"Hey," Harvey yelled, "I've got this great idea!"